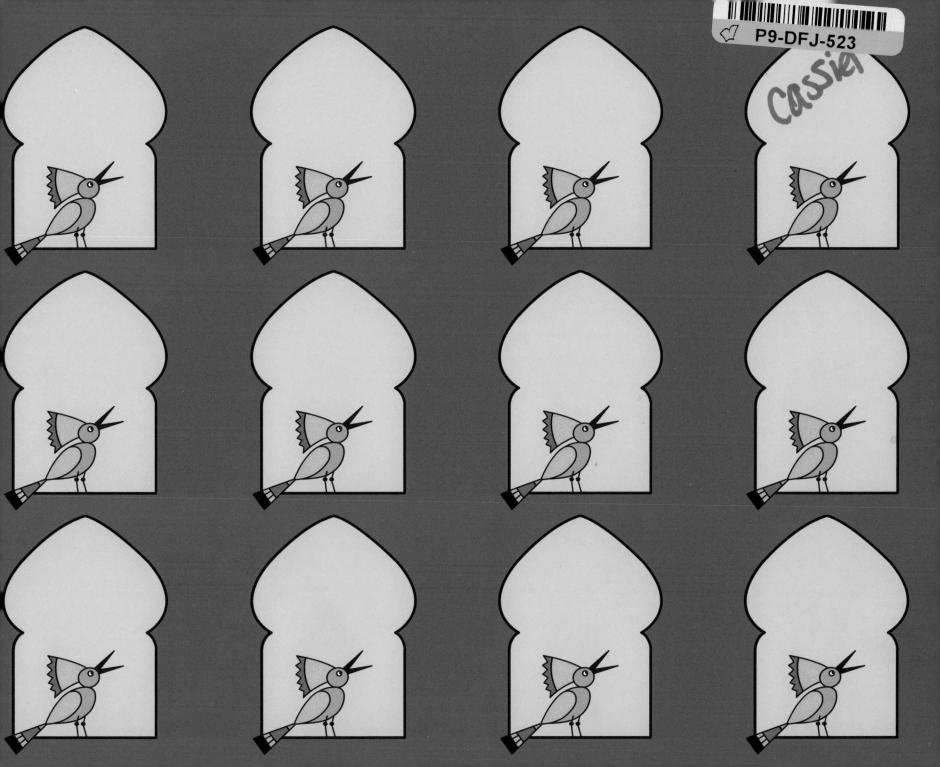

Cassie

The Girl who Lost Her Smile

For Jemana—Karim

For Aniela Woodward—Stefan

Text copyright © 2000 by Karim Alrawi
Illustration copyright © 2000 by Stefan Czernecki
Published simultaneously in Canada by Tradewind Books, Ltd.
Printed in Hong Kong
First Edition

Library of Congress Cataloging-in-Publication Data
Alrawi, Karim.
The girl who lost her smile / written by Karim Alrawi; illustrated by Stefan Czernecki—
1st ed.
p. cm
Summary: A story about a young Persian girl who unexpectedly finds reason to smile,
inspired by the writings of Jallal al-Din Rumi in a collection of Sufi poetry and short stories known as Mathnawi.
ISBN 1-890817-17-1
[1. Persia Fiction.] I. Czernecki, Stefan, ill. II. Title.
PZ7.A4626 Gi 2000
[E] – dc21
99-462308   CIP

Prepress work by Supreme Graphics, Burnaby, British Columbia

Designers:
Rose Walsh
Andrew Johnstone
Adrienne Mason

For games, links and more, visit our interactive Web site:
www.winslowpress.com

The Girl who Lost Her Smile

Written by Karim Alrawi
Illustrated by Stefan Czernecki

WINSLOW PRESS

Delray Beach, Florida • New York

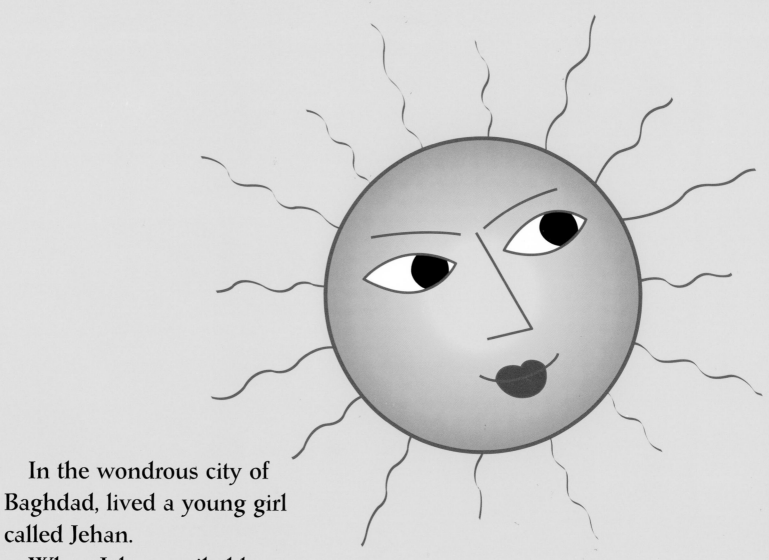

In the wondrous city of Baghdad, lived a young girl called Jehan.

When Jehan smiled by day, the sun shone brightly.

When she smiled at night, the stars glittered and sparkled.

One dull morning, she woke up and could not find her smile. She looked under the bed and in the closet. She looked all over the house and in the garden, but she could not find her smile anywhere.

The people of Baghdad
looked up at the sky but
could not see the sun.
    "We must help Jehan find
her smile," they said.
    The
jugglers
juggled and
the fire-eaters
bellowed flames, but still
Jehan could not find her
smile.

"Oh, dear," she said. "I'll never smile again."

"What can we do to help Jehan?" her father asked the hoopoe, a small, but very wise bird, as they sat together one night under a mangrove tree.

The hoopoe ruffled his crown of golden feathers. "What if we invited the greatest artists in the world to paint pictures for her?"

The Italian artists came
across the sea in ships
with fluttering sails.
They painted the
ceiling with laughing
cherubim and singing
seraphim.

"It's beautiful," said Jehan.

But still she could not find her smile.

The Chinese artists came with wagons of paint across mountain peaks of glittering ice. They painted the walls with imaginary beasts and wondrous dragons.

"It's beautiful," said Jehan.

So, the hoopoe set off in search of an artist who could help Jehan find her smile.

He traveled to the monasteries of Tibet. "Too scary," he said.

He flew over the pyramids of Egypt.
"Too serious," he chirped.

On his way back, the
hoopoe stopped in Persia.

"I'll never be able to help
Jehan find her smile," he
sighed.

Just then a young man heard the hoopoe. He asked the little bird why he was so sad. The hoopoe told him his story. "I think I can help your friend find her smile," said the young man.

When the young
Persian and the hoopoe
arrived at Jehan's home,
all he had with him was
a small leather pouch.

"I've found the man
who'll help you find your
smile," said the hoopoe,
fluttering his wings. "I'm
sure I have."

The Persian took a
simple sandalwood scraper
out of his bag. Very gently,
he started to smooth the wall.

"Please help me," said the Persian as he handed Jehan a scraper.

It was hard work
smoothing the wall, and at
first, Jehan felt tired. But as
she polished and cleaned,
the work became easier
and easier.

Soon the wall began to glow, and Jehan saw that its beauty had always been there. It had just been waiting for her to uncover it. Jehan began to smile.

The more she smiled,
the brighter the wall
became, until it was as
glorious as a summer's day.

Outside, the people of
Baghdad looked up and
saw that the sun was now
shining.

"At last," they said, "Jehan has found her smile."

Author's Note:

The Girl Who Lost Her Smile was inspired by a story in the collection of short stories and poetry called *Mathnawi* by Jallal al-Din Rumi

Jallal al-Din Rumi was a mystical teacher, poet and storyteller who lived in the Turkish city of Konya. He was the founder of the order of the Whirling Dervish, who use music and dance to achieve a mystical state of worship. The order continues to this day.

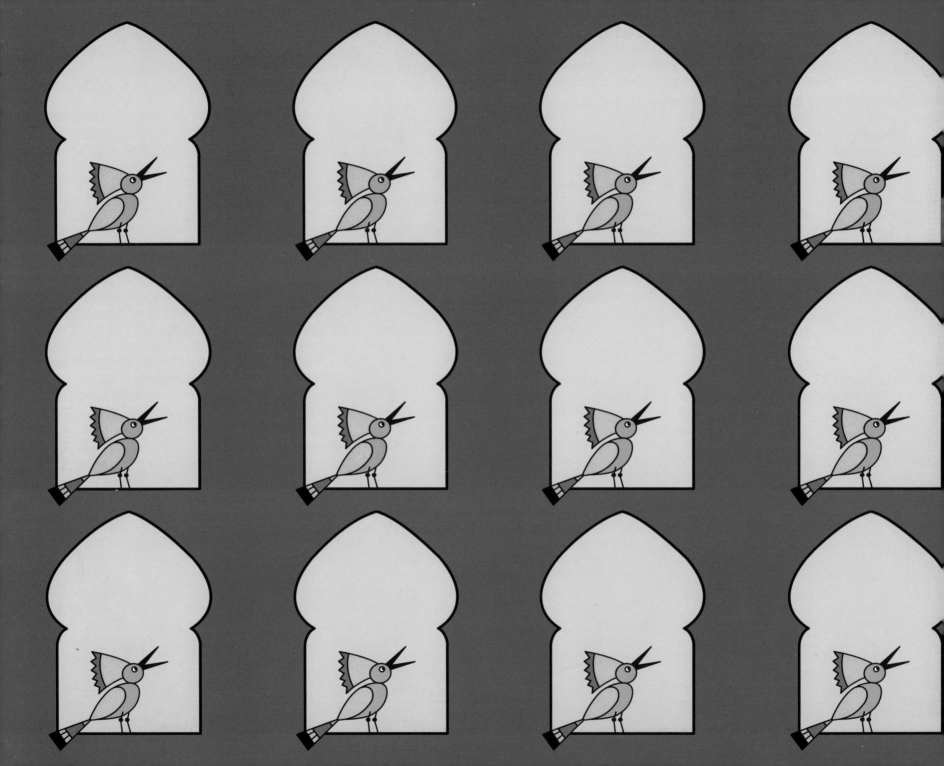